Stingo's Sneaky Picnic

★ Created by Keith Chapman ★

First published in the UK by HarperCollins Children's Books in 2010

1 3 5 7 9 10 8 6 4 2
ISBN: 978-0-00-734699-8

A CIP catalogue record for this title is available from the British Library.

Based on the television series Fifi and the Flowertots and the original script 'Naughty Twins' by Wayne Jackman.
Adapted for this publication by Mandy Archer.
© Chapman Entertainment Limited 2010
Printed and bound in China

Stingo's Sneaky Picnic

HarperCollins *Children's Books*

Fifi had decided to spend
the morning picking blackberries.
She drove Mo to the meadow, then
waited for Buttercup and Daisy to arrive.
"Sorry we're late!" waved Buttercup,
as Flutterby bumped into view.
"Whoopsy Daisy!" cried Daisy.
"Hello!" smiled Fifi, handing the Tots a basket
each. "Are you ready to start picking?"

The meadow was full of juicy, ripe berries. They looked so
yummy that Buttercup and Daisy couldn't help eating a few!
Fifi looked at their juice-stained faces and sighed.
"Fiddly Flowerpetals! We're not going to have enough
blackberries to bake tarts at this rate."
"Sorry Fifi," giggled the twins.

Over at the market, Stingo and Slugsy were also feeling peckish. "I'm starving," grumbled Stingo. "I haven't had a decent meal since my second breakfast this morning!"

When the pair strolled past Poppy's stall, Stingo's eyes lit up. Four delicious-looking apple pies were lined up in neat rows. "Pity we haven't got any money to buy one, eh bosss?" sighed Slugsy. Stingo ignored him and shouted for Poppy. "Could we have a couple of those pies?" he asked. "I'll pay you later, promise." Poppy shook her head. "You still haven't paid for the last lot. Hop it Stingo!"

Stingo decided to look elsewhere. He tried
grabbing a batch of Aunt Tulip's flapjacks, but
she shooed the naughty wasp away. Next
they tried Violet and Primrose's house.
"I spy fairy cakes!" cheered Stingo,
pointing to their garden table.
"Nip in and take them, Slugsy."

Slugsy felt uneasy,
but orders were orders.
He slithered into the
garden and started
to help himself.
Just then, Primrose
opened the front door.
"After our cakes
I suppose?" she frowned.
"See yourself out!"

Back at the meadow, Buttercup and Daisy
were getting tired of picking blackberries.
"Catch!" cried Daisy, tossing a berry to her sister.

Jumping geraniums!

gasped Fifi. "You're covered in sticky juice."
There was nothing for it – the twins would have
to go home and get cleaned up. The Tots grabbed
their blackberry baskets
and scampered onto Flutterby.

As soon as they got back to Milk
Bucket House, the twins raced inside.
"Come on Daisy!" urged Buttercup.
"Race you to the bathroom."
Just at that moment, Stingo
and Slugsy slunk past.
"Look at those blackberries!"
whispered Slugsy, pointing
at the baskets.

Stingo crept forward and grabbed a basket,
just as Buttercup and Daisy came back outside.
Under their arms the sisters cuddled their
favourite toys – Cornflower and Diddyduck.
"Stingo!" said Daisy. "Those blackberries
are for Fifi's tarts."

Stingo suddenly began to smirk.
"Ah erm, yes," he began. "Fifi has asked me to organise a picnic for all
the Tots in the garden. She told me to collect these blackberries for it."
The twins cheered. "Can we help too?"
Stingo nodded. "The Flowertots have left picnic food out all over
the garden, will you fetch it for me?"

Stingo told Slugsy to show the twins where to find the goodies, while he buzzed off home. The sneaky wasp wanted everything delivered to Apple Tree House. Slugsy sighed. He knew what they were doing was wrong, but Stingo wouldn't take no for an answer. First stop on the list was Poppy's stall.

"Look Daisy," said Buttercup when they got to the market. "Poppy has left apple pies out for the picnic." Slugsy felt very guilty as the little Tot took a pie and handed it to him. "We're doing a really good job, aren't we?" beamed Daisy.

The friends walked on through the garden.

"Look!" cooed Daisy. "Aunt Tulip has made flapjacks for the picnic!" She scampered onto Aunt Tulip's veranda and helped herself to a big plateful. She was so thrilled with the flapjacks, poor Diddyduck got dropped on the floor!

Primrose and Violet's cottage was next. Slugsy hung back outside the gate, while the twins picked the fairy cakes off the table. Buttercup let go of Cornflower and smiled. "These cakes will be lovely to have at the picnic!"

Stingo watched the twins through his spyglass. He could hardly believe his luck!

"Sting-a-Ling!"

he cackled, as Buttercup and Daisy laid the feast out on a picnic rug at the bottom of his tree.

Buttercup stood on her tiptoes and shouted up to the branches. "Is there anything else we can do to help with the picnic Stingo?" The wasp searched the garden until he spotted some honeypots sitting on Bumble's doorstep. He grinned naughtily then sent his helpers over to get them too.

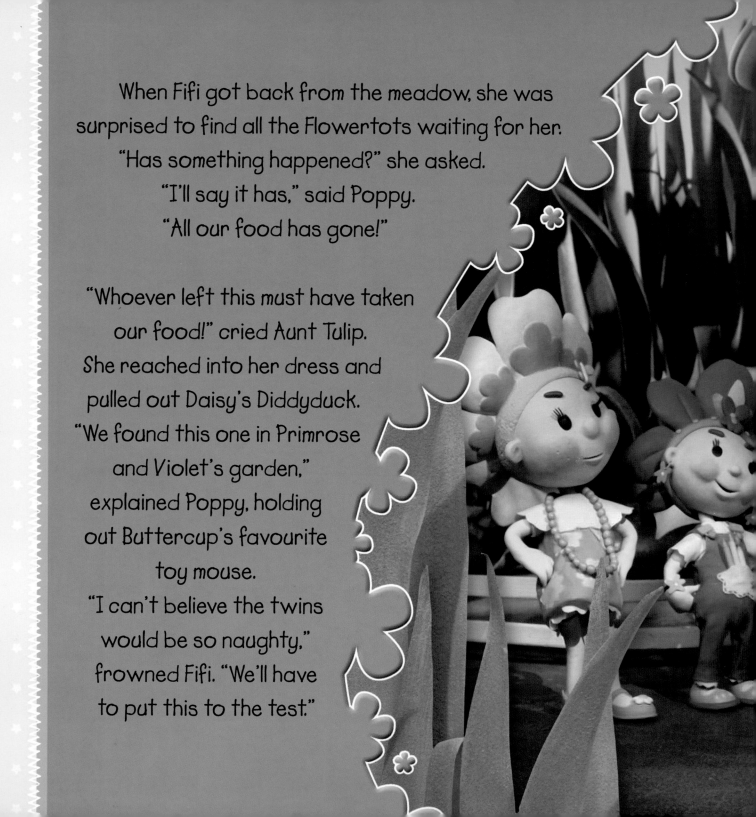

When Fifi got back from the meadow, she was surprised to find all the Flowertots waiting for her. "Has something happened?" she asked.
"I'll say it has," said Poppy.
"All our food has gone!"

"Whoever left this must have taken our food!" cried Aunt Tulip. She reached into her dress and pulled out Daisy's Diddyduck. "We found this one in Primrose and Violet's garden," explained Poppy, holding out Buttercup's favourite toy mouse. "I can't believe the twins would be so naughty," frowned Fifi. "We'll have to put this to the test."

Fifi placed a basket of blackberries outside her front door, then told everyone to hide. A few minutes later, Buttercup and Daisy trotted up to Forget-me-not Cottage, closely followed by Slugsy.

"Here's some more fruit for the picnic," laughed Daisy. "Let's get it."

Fifi and her friends stood up at once. Everyone looked very disappointed.

"Buttercup and Daisy!" gasped Fifi. "Why have you been taking everyone's food?"

"It's for the Tots' picnic," answered Buttercup.

Slugsy flushed bright red. "Don't blame the twins, Fifi! Ssstingo pretended there was a picnic ssso he could trick them into taking all of your treatsss."

"I see," said Fifi. "I think we need to have a word with Stingo."

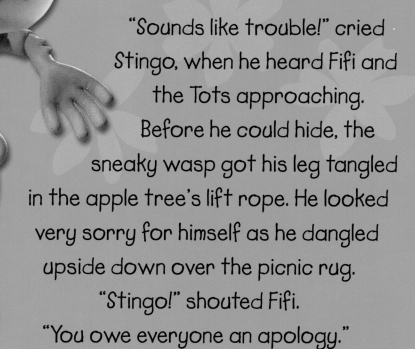

"Sounds like trouble!" cried
Stingo, when he heard Fifi and
the Tots approaching.
Before he could hide, the
sneaky wasp got his leg tangled
in the apple tree's lift rope. He looked
very sorry for himself as he dangled
upside down over the picnic rug.
"Stingo!" shouted Fifi.
"You owe everyone an apology."
The wasp fell to the ground with a big bump!
"I... I... I'm really sorry," he said meekly.

Once Stingo had been forgiven, Bumble had a
great idea. "Why don't we have a picnic now?"
Everyone cheered. Fifi told Stingo to swing the rope
so that the twins could skip.
"Faster Stingo!" she grinned. "As you like playing tricks
so much, you can do this for the rest of the afternoon!"

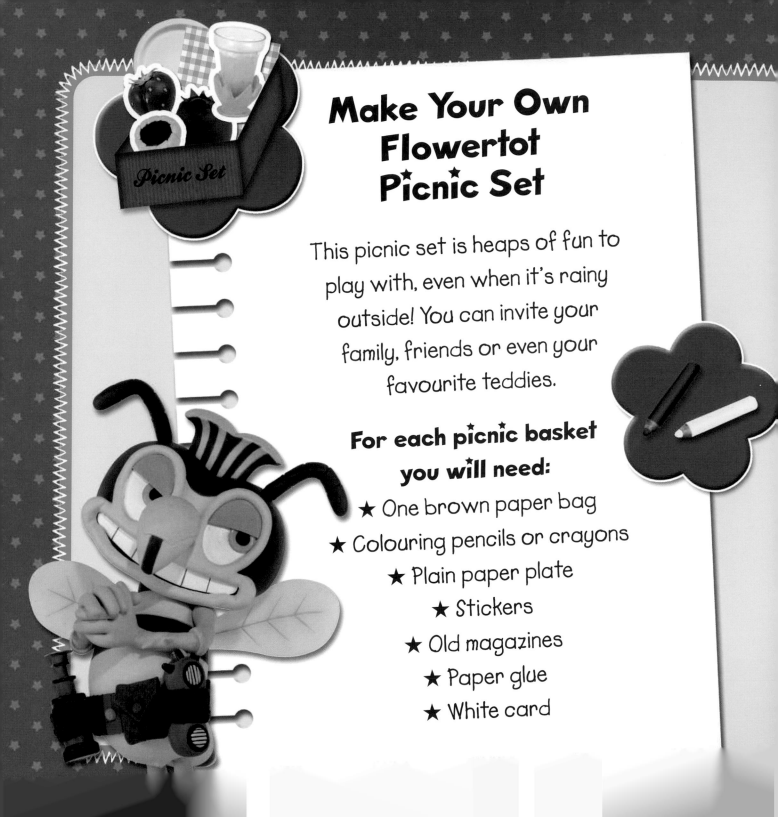

Make Your Own Flowertot Picnic Set

This picnic set is heaps of fun to play with, even when it's rainy outside! You can invite your family, friends or even your favourite teddies.

For each picnic basket you will need:

★ One brown paper bag

★ Colouring pencils or crayons

★ Plain paper plate

★ Stickers

★ Old magazines

★ Paper glue

★ White card

Picnic Set

1. Ask a grown-up to cut the top half off a brown paper bag so that it makes a shallow basket shape.

2. Use a brown pencil or crayon to draw criss-cross basket lines over the bag.

3. Take the paper plate and write your name on the front in neat letters. Now use coloured pencils or crayons to decorate the rest of the plate in a pretty design. Tuck the finished plate in your picnic basket.

4. Flick through some old magazines, collecting pictures of your favourite foods. Don't forget to look for some healthy fruit, some sandwiches or pasta, a drink and a sweet treat to nibble!

5. Ask a grown-up to cut out all your picnic food and stick each item on a sheet of white card.

6. Ask a grown-up to cut each of the mounted food pieces out and pop them into your basket. Now you're ready to lay a rug on the floor and play flowertot picnics!

ALWAYS ASK A GROWN-UP
TO HELP YOU WITH SCISSORS

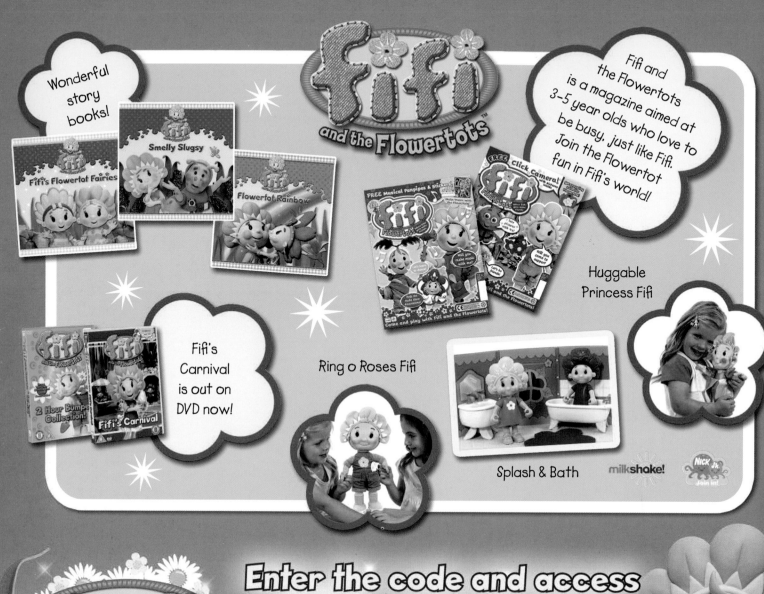

Wonderful story books!

Fifi's Flowertot Fairies

Smelly Slugsy

Flowertot Rainbow

Fifi and the Flowertots is a magazine aimed at 3–5 year olds who love to be busy, just like Fifi. Join the Flowertot fun in Fifi's world!

FREE Musical Panpipes & Stickers!

FREE click Camera!

Huggable Princess Fifi

Fifi's Carnival is out on DVD now!

2 Hour Bumper Collection!

Fifi's Carnival

Ring o Roses Fifi

Splash & Bath

milkshake!

NICK Jr. Join in!